Why Me?

Positive Verse for Loss & Sadness
For Ages 3 & Up

Written & Illustrated by
Phebe Phillips

Story originally written for use by chapters of the American Red Cross.

HGP

Library of Congress Control Number Data
Phillips, Phebe
Why Me? Positive Verse for Loss and Sadness / Written & Illustrated by Phebe Philips, —1st ed.
Summary: Soothing words of comfort for both the child and adult reader as they are guided through life's sometimes catastrophic events.
Why Me? Positive Verse for Loss and Sadness / Phebe Phillips.
1. Family—Growing Up & Facts of Life—Children's Books.
2. Self-Esteem & Self-Respect—Growing Up & Facts of Life—Children's Books.
Fiction. | BISAC: JUVENILE / Social Situations / General. | Juvenile / Social Situation / New Experience | SELF-HELP / Death, Grief, Bereavement | BODY, MIND & SPIRIT / Inspiration & Personal Growth 2018
Library of Congress 201707384
First Edition.
ISBN: 9780983782032 (IngramSpark, Soft Cover)
ISBN: 9780983782025 (IngramSpark, Hard Cover)
ISBN: 9780983782049 (CreateSpace, Soft Cover)

The illustrations in this book were rendered in chalk pastel.
The cover text was set in Omnes Bold. The storybook text was set in Museo Sans Rounded.
Book design by Taylor Davis at Sundaram in Austin, Texas.

Why Me? Positive Verse for Loss and Sadness guides young and old readers through life's sometimes catastrophic events. Why Me? is designed to bring words of comfort to those affected by life-changing events such as a death, the heart-breaking loss of a pet, a change in family structure or one of life's many challenges and disappointments.

Phebe Phillips is a Texas author best known for her past creations of exquisite stuffed toys sold for twenty-five-years at Neiman Marcus and other retailers. In her children's stories her work explores positive themes of growth, happiness and overcoming limitation. Like her past toy line, her themes are designed for children, yet possess an intellectual depth appealing to adults.

Contact Phebe
P.O. Box 190748
Dallas, Texas 75219
U.S.A.
phebe@phebephillips.com
www.phebephillips.com

Why me... me, me?

I'm sad, I'm mad.

I used to be happy,

I used to be glad.

I'm afraid, I feel pain.

I want my world back.

I want it the same!

Why did this happen? Please tell me now.
Can someone explain? Am I to blame?

You're not to blame and you
should never feel shame.

Sometimes life changes with
a flame or a flood. Sometimes
it's wind and a great big THUD!

Sometimes the body can get very ill, making you swallow

a great BIG PILL.

Sometimes things leave...
gone for good.
If only, if only, this could be
understood.

People want to help and answer your cries,
but sometimes they don't even know why.
They scratch their heads and imagine your pain.
This pain, from which you have much to gain.

There are breaks of the bones,
and breaks of the heart.
Both can give you a fresh new start.

The Earth is watered,
new growth comes with rain.
You and Earth are a lot the same.
Tears water your heart so you can grow,
and in your heart you begin to know...

It's okay to be sad or mad or afraid.
It's okay to think back to that perfect day.
Your world was nice, everything was in place,
but now you have a chance for a brand new space.

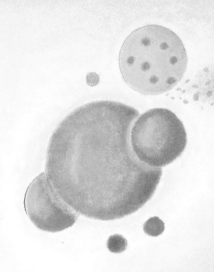

New space where you live.

New space in your heart.

New space that comes from a

promising new start.

Sometimes the worst happens to the best.
Sometimes the most special get put to the test.
These are the things that make you unlike the rest.
These are the things that can bring out your best.

Your life is a story with good and bad.
Your life is a book both happy and sad.

Your world will get better.
Someday, coming soon.
Till then remember to wish on the moon.

You have a choice to be mad or glad.
You have a choice to be happy or sad.
Choose the light little friend,
be happy with glee!
It may take some work to get there,
you'll see...

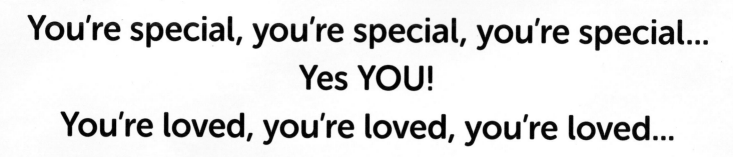

You're special, you're special, you're special...
Yes YOU!
You're loved, you're loved, you're loved...
and this is true.